DC SUPER HEROES

ROBIN™

AN ORIGIN STORY

raintree
a Capstone company — publishers for children

Raintree is an imprint of Capstone Global Library Limited, a company
incorporated in England and Wales having its registered office at 264
Banbury Road, Oxford, OX2 7DY – Registered company number: 6695582

www.raintree.co.uk
myorders@raintree.co.uk

Designed by Hilary Wacholz
Contributing artists: Luciano Vecchio, Dan Schoenin, Erik Doescher,
Mike DeCarlo, Lee Loughridge and Leonel Castellani
Printed and bound in India

978 1 3982 0604 5 (hardback)
978 1 3982 0605 2 (paperback)

British Library Cataloguing in Publication Data
A full catalogue record for this book is available from the British Library.

AN ORIGIN STORY

WRITTEN BY
MICHAEL DAHL

ILLUSTRATED BY
DARIO BRIZUELA

BATMAN CREATED BY
BOB KANE WITH BILL FINGER

One night, young Tim Drake and his family are in the city.

Police sirens are ringing through the night. Tim sees two shadows high overhead. It is Batman and Robin.

They are chasing the Penguin.
The **villain** is on the roof of a tall
building. He carries a bag full of
stolen jewels.

A guard on the roof jumps towards the Penguin. He misses and falls!

Robin sees the falling guard. The young hero swings on his rope towards the man.

Is he too far away to help?

Robin lets go of his rope. He flips through the air four times. The flip carries him further.

Robin reaches out. He catches
the man.

The Boy Wonder lands lightly on the ground. The guard is safe.

Everyone cheers!

Tim Drake cheers the loudest. No one else can do Robin's special **quadruple** flip!

An idea pops into Tim's clever brain. He thinks he knows something about the Boy Wonder.

When Tim and his parents get home, Tim runs to his room.

The boy is a brilliant student. He knows everything about the two heroes. His bedroom walls are covered with posters of Batman and Robin.

Tim remembers a story he once read. Years ago, a circus visited the city. The star performers were a family of **acrobats**. They were called the Flying Graysons.

The youngest acrobat, Dick Grayson, performed an amazing stunt. He flipped through the air four times in a row.

Only two people have ever done that amazing flip successfully – Dick Grayson and Robin.

Dick's parents were later killed in a circus accident. Then the boy was **adopted** by billionaire Bruce Wayne.

Tim thinks that Bruce and Dick are the **Dynamic** Duo. But he never tells anyone the heroes' secret.

As Tim grows older, so does Robin.

Robin is a young man. He becomes a new hero, Nightwing.

Nightwing protects Gotham City just like Batman. But the two men don't always work together.

Batman no longer has a young partner by his side.

As a teenager, Tim Drake has another brilliant idea.

He visits the home of Bruce Wayne.

"I know your secret," Tim says. "I know that you are Batman. I know that Dick Grayson is Nightwing."

Tim sticks out his chest, proudly. "I want to be your new Robin," he says.

Bruce Wayne smiles.

"You're very clever to have figured that out," he says. "Let me show you another secret."

Bruce takes Tim down a special elevator. At the bottom, Tim sees a gigantic cave.

"The Batcave!" he says.

"You could be a great Robin," says Bruce. "But my partner must have special training."

Tim is excited. "I'll do whatever it takes," Tim says. He is also **determined** to do his best.

"Then we begin today," says Bruce.

Tim Drake goes on a busy tour around the globe.

He works with the best teachers and trainers.

Tim learns **martial arts**.

He works on acrobatic tricks. He discovers how to escape from traps.

And, most importantly, he learns how to track down criminals.

When he has finished training, Tim returns to the Batcave. He shows Batman the skills he has learned.

Batman has a surprise too.

"A new Robin costume!" says Tim.

"And you will be the first to wear it," says Batman.

A light flashes in the Batcave.

"Someone needs our help," says Batman.

This is it, thinks Tim.

Tim rides in the Batmobile for the first time. Batman drives to a hotel that towers high in the sky.

"Going up!" says Batman.

The two heroes fling their Batarangs and hook onto the building. Swiftly, they climb up the glassy side.

Near the top of the building they hear shouts and screams.

A crowd of people is trapped in a giant ballroom. Their feet are stuck in slimy goo.

"Hand over your money and your jewels!" cries a strange, muddy figure.

"It's Clayface!" says Batman.

Batman lets go of his Batrope and leaps into the room. But Clayface spies him. His gloppy arm grows long and reaches towards the Dark Knight.

Batman slips on the goo. Clayface pushes him backwards. Batman begins to fall.

"Batman!" shouts Tim.

Tim slips down his long rope.

He leaps.

He flips over and over. He flips four times!

The flips give him extra speed. Tim swoops in and catches Batman's hand.

Then Tim throws another Batarang.

It wraps around a nearby pole and the heroes swing to safety.

"Well done," says Batman. "Only one person can do that trick."

"I guess that means I'm Robin," says Tim, hopefully

Batman smiles.

"It means you're a hero, Tim," says the Dark Knight. "Now, let's go and get Clayface!"

37

The heroes climb back into the building. Clayface is still robbing the people in the ballroom. He is not happy to see the heroes again.

But, working together, Batman and Robin are able to defeat him.

The Dynamic Duo turn the captured Clayface over to the police.

Before they can be thanked, the two heroes disappear into the shadows. There is always another villain in Gotham City who needs to be stopped.

Batman no longer works alone. He has a true partner by his side.

Robin, the Boy Wonder!

ROBIN

REAL NAME: TIM DRAKE

ROLE: CRIME FIGHTER AND BATMAN'S SIDEKICK

BASE: GOTHAM CITY

Tim Drake figured out Batman's secret, and wanted to be a part of it. After intense training to become Gotham City's next super hero, he was granted the honour of wearing his very own Robin costume.

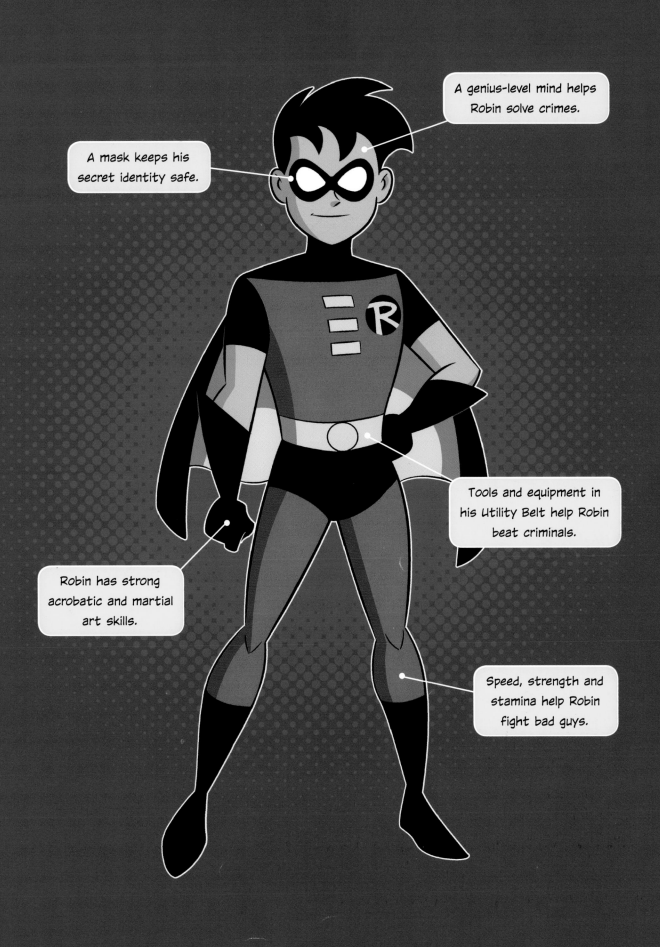

A genius-level mind helps Robin solve crimes.

A mask keeps his secret identity safe.

Tools and equipment in his Utility Belt help Robin beat criminals.

Robin has strong acrobatic and martial art skills.

Speed, strength and stamina help Robin fight bad guys.

THE AUTHOR

MICHAEL DAHL is the prolific author of the bestselling *Goodnight, Baseball* picture book and more than 200 other books for children and young adults. He has won the AEP Distinguished Achievement Award three times for his non-fiction, a Teacher's Choice award from Learning magazine and a Seal of Excellence from the Creative Child Awards. Dahl currently lives in Minneapolis, Minnesota, USA.

THE ILLUSTRATOR

DARIO BRIZUELA was born in Buenos Aires, Argentina, and as a teen he began studying in an art school – doing drawing, sculpture, painting and more. After discovering super hero comic books, his goal was draw his favourite characters. He has worked for major publishers like Dark Horse Comics, IDW, Viz Media, DC Comics and Marvel Comics. He has also worked for Hasbro and LEGO. Star Wars Tales, Super Friends, Justice League Unlimited and Scooby-Doo are just a few of his artistic contributions.

GLOSSARY

acrobat a person who performs gymnastics acts that require great skill

adopt to take as one's own

determined having a firm or fixed purpose

dynamic positive in attitude and full of new energy and new ideas

martial arts a style of fighting or self-defence that comes mostly from the Far East

quadruple four of a thing

villain a wicked, evil or bad person who is often a character in a story

DISCUSSION QUESTIONS

Write down your answers. Refer back to the story for help.

QUESTION 1.

Reread pages 20-21. What skills did Tim learn? Flip back through the book and look at the illustrations. Can you find any pictures that match the descriptions?

QUESTION 2.

Robin's signature move is a quadruple flip. Do you know of any other characters who have a signature move?

QUESTION 3.

Look at the picture on page 19. Describe the Batcave. What is it like? What other interesting things do you think are inside?

READ THEM ALL!!

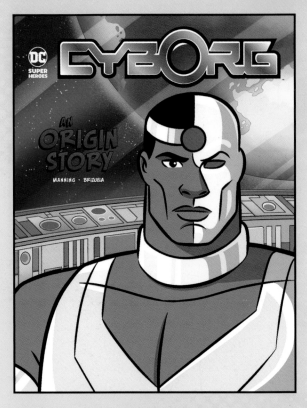